# EGYPTIAN
# MYTHOLOGY

JANELL BROYLES

rosen
central™

The Rosen Publishing Group, Inc., New York

Published in 2006 by The Rosen Publishing Group, Inc.
29 East 21st Street, New York, NY 10010

Copyright © 2006 by The Rosen Publishing Group, Inc.

First Edition

**Library of Congress Cataloging-in-Publication Data**

Broyles, Janell.
Egyptian mythology/Janell Broyles.—1st ed.
    p. cm.—(Mythology around the world)
Includes bibliographical references and index.
ISBN 1-4042-0770-8 (library binding)
1. Mythology, Egyptian—Juvenile literature. 2. Egypt—Religious life and customs—Juvenile literature.
I. Title. II. Series.
BL2441.2.B76 2005
299'.3113—dc22

                                                                2005014610

*Manufactured in the United States of America*

**On the cover:** Painting of Atum and Osiris from the tomb of Nefertari.

# CONTENTS

# INTRODUCTION: "WONDERFUL THINGS"

On November 26, 1922, the archaeologist Howard Carter stood before a sealed stone door in Egypt's Valley of the Kings. He didn't know if he would find a king's tomb on the other side or merely a plundered storage room. It was a painstaking process to clear the rubble away from the door, revealing the seals that bore the name of King Tutankhamen. Carter made a tiny hole in the door's corner, held up a candle, and peered inside. According to *The Discovery of the Tomb of Tutankhamen*, his companion asked excitedly, "Can you see anything?" Carter, seeing the glitter of countless gold and jeweled artifacts—the treasures of a pharaoh, miraculously preserved—answered, "Yes. Wonderful things."

The discovery of Tutankhamen's tomb, with its amazing treasures, reignited the West's interest in ancient Egypt. While many tombs and monuments had been explored already, this tomb offered a uniquely comprehensive look at the sophisticated and powerful ancient Egyptian culture. A fad for Egyptian culture influenced jewelry, fashion, and even books and movies in the West. It's a fad that continues today, in the form of movies such as *The Mummy* and the imitations of monuments like the Great Sphinx of Giza and the pyramids in places such as Las Vegas, Nevada.

Ancient Egypt fascinates us because it was such a rich and advanced culture, yet we still know so little about it. Thanks to the hieroglyphs and scrolls left behind by its scribes and artists, we have a basic understanding of Egyptian religion, myths, and daily life.

But there are still a great many gaps in our knowledge. How many stories, songs, myths, and legends were told around hearths or before pharaohs and were never written down? In addition, there still remain tombs and burial places unexplored or covered by the desert sand, waiting to be discovered. Perhaps there are myths and legends that remain to be found that will help us understand more about the ancient Egyptians and their perception of their world.

In the following chapters, we will explore what we do know about Egyptian mythology and daily life, and investigate some of the universal fears, hopes, and truths that their mythology—like all mythologies—tried to explain.

**Shown here is the most accurate re-creation of the appearance of King Tut on the day he died, as created by three forensic teams from France, America, and Egypt on May 10, 2005.**

5

# 1 ANCIENT EGYPTIAN CULTURE

There is evidence that human beings lived and traveled through the area we now call Egypt for thousands of years before any advanced civilizations began to form. Eventually, villages, and then cities, arose on the fertile Nile plain, and around 3000 BC, the First Dynasty began the long age of Egyptian power.

The Nile's fertile plain was the source of Egypt's riches. The regular flooding of the Nile made the area around it an oasis in a harsh desert, dumping rich soil on its banks. Sometimes the floods also took many lives when they were too fierce, or caused starvation when they were too weak.

In addition, the Nile was relatively easy to travel, making it simpler for rulers to control all

This pyramidion, or capstone of a pyramid, shows the falcon god Horus.

This fifteenth-century mural is from the eighteenth Egyptian dynasty. The mural is from the tomb of Sennefer, mayor of Thebes during the reign of Amenophis II, and depicts boatmen sailing up the Nile. The Nile was a major source of food and means of travel for the ancient Egyptians.

the people who lived up and down its length and for trade to thrive. Wild game was abundant. Wood was scarce, but in the dry climate, mud bricks worked perfectly well for everyday housing. For grand temples and tombs, there was sandstone and limestone, although quarrying and transporting blocks of stone required enormous manpower. As Egypt grew in power, traders from nearby lands brought jewels, exotic animals, and other luxuries to sell to wealthy nobility.

# The Structure of Egyptian Society

At the bottom of Egyptian society were slaves and servants, many times brought from distant lands or captured in battle. In the service of a nobleman, they might be freed or at least given great responsibility, but like all slaves, they had little say in how they lived.

Next were the farmers, simple men and women who worked on the land owned by the nobility. They lived in small mud-brick houses and paid taxes on the crops and livestock they raised. Their lives were broken into three seasons: inundation, when the Nile flooded their lands; planting, when the waters withdrew and left the soil moist enough to be seeded; and harvest.

There was a social structure in ancient Egypt just as there is in societies today. Shown here is a fourteenth-century wall painting from the tomb of Unsou. It shows people, who are likely slaves, loading grain onto a ship, most likely for travel up the Nile.

Above them were the artisans and craftsmen, those who carved the great statues and monuments, painted the elaborate tombs, and made everything from simple pottery to the pharaoh's throne. Although the work they left behind often showed great beauty and skill, their names were not recorded because artisans were not considered of particularly high status.

Next were the scribes, who might work in an obscure village storehouse or in the presence of the pharaoh himself. The invention of paper, in the form of papyrus, allowed the Egyptians to keep elaborate and accurate records of crops raised, tributes gathered, laws, and the great deeds of the pharaoh. Even more valuable, scribes would sometimes write down more personal details. These details included trading trips taken, or myths, stories, poetry, and songs, giving us a window into everyday Egyptian life. Becoming a scribe was one of the few ways to move up in Egyptian society. A clever scribe might attach himself to a powerful noble and gain a great deal of responsibility, wealth, and power.

The nobility and the priests formed the next layer of Egyptian society, just below the pharaoh himself. All land supposedly belonged to the pharaohs, but as Egyptian society grew, the pharaohs were forced to delegate responsibilities to trusted family members, giving them access to wealth and power, and if they were lucky, making their children eligible for marriage into the royal family itself. Originally, the priests owned no land. In the later dynasties, though, some temples were given tributes of wealth and land by the pharaohs who made the most powerful priests equal in the nobility.

In addition to the Egyptian pharaoh being considered the living embodiment of the gods, he, and occasionally she, was treated with the greatest respect, both in life and in death. Shown here is the god Horus performing the opening-of-the-mouth ceremony on the recently deceased Ramses II. This ceremony was performed to prepare the deceased for the journey into the afterlife.

At the top of Egyptian society was the pharaoh and his family. Considered the living embodiment of the god Horus, one of the greatest gods in the Egyptian pantheon, the pharaoh was worshipped as a god himself. Inheritance of the crown passed from father to son or, rarely, to daughter. Pharaohs usually married their own sisters or half sisters, on the assumption that it was best to marry someone equally royal.

# The Egyptian Family

Egyptians were patriarchal, meaning that the husband or oldest male was the head of the household and had final say in all decisions. This is how it was in most ancient societies. Marriages were often arranged by the parents of the couple, who had little say in the matter. In practice, some marriages may have been relatively happy—bits of advice preserved on papyri have come down to us recommending that a husband treat his wife with respect and honor in order to have a happy home.

Children were cherished. Later Greek observers were surprised that Egypt's bounty allowed families to raise all the children who were born, unlike the harsher climate of Greece, where some families were forced to abandon infants they could not afford to feed. Families were attached to the land on which they lived. Land owned by a noble and containing his family, their servants, farmers, and artisans formed a largely self-sufficient community that grew its own food and made its own clothing and necessities. Unless traveling for trade or festivals, Egyptians tended to stay close to home.

# A Brief Overview of Egyptian History

Egypt's history as an empire lasted more than 3,000 years, so there is not enough space here to cover it in great detail. But to understand its myths and culture, it helps to have a basic idea of the major periods during this reign. There is much debate over the

**Shown here are the ruins of Tanis, which may have once been the capital Avaris of the Hyksos rulers, who ruled during the Second Intermediate Period. An important center, the area was strewn with statues, inscriptions, obelisks, and reliefs.**

dates of the time periods, but the following is one account:

- Predynastic Period (before 3000 BC): The period of time before there was any organized Egyptian state.

- Early Dynastic Period (3000–2625 BC): The earliest Egyptian government included the First and Second dynasties.

- Old Kingdom (2625–2130 BC): The first peak of Egyptian culture, lasting until the invasion of the Hyksos conquerors. This included the Third through the Eighth dynasties.

- First Intermediate Period (2130–1980 BC): This included the Ninth and Tenth dynasties.

- Middle Kingdom (1980–1630 BC): The second great period of Egyptian culture after the invaders were cast out. This included the Eleventh through Thirteenth dynasties.

- Second Intermediate Period (1630–1539 BC): This was the period of struggle against the Hyksos, who ruled in the north-eastern Nile delta and comprised the Fifteenth Dynasty.

- New Kingdom (1539–1075 BC): The third and final great period of ancient Egyptian culture. This included the reign of famous rulers such as Amenhotep III, Nefertiti, Tutankhamen, and Ramses II. It ended with the Twentieth Dynasty.

- Third Intermediate Period (1075–525 BC): Dynasties Twenty-one through Twenty-six. Includes rule by foreigners including the Libyans and Nubians.

- Late Period (525–332 BC): Dynasties Twenty-seven through Thirty-one. Includes two periods when Egypt was ruled by the Persians as well as the last native Egyptian pharaoh, Nectanebo II of the Thirtieth Dynasty.

- Greco-Roman Period (332 BC–AD 395).

Egypt's ancient language was eventually partially subsumed under Greek, Latin, and finally Arabic. Many of the great tombs were robbed of their treasures and became curiosities for Greek and Roman tourists, who went so far as to scribble their names inside the sacred resting places of pharaohs. The old gods were neglected and finally given up for the newer gods of the Greeks and Romans,

In Egyptian mythology, the sphinx, a creature with a lion's body and a human head, is an important figure. The Great Sphinx in Giza, Egypt, shown here, is one of the most recognizable of ancient Egyptian relics. It dates from the reign of King Khafre of the Fourth Dynasty and is believed to be a portrait of the king himself.

and then of Christianity and Islam. During the nineteenth century, French soldiers even used the Great Sphinx for target practice with their rifles. We owe a great deal to the scholars, such as Herodotus, who wrote down what they could of the rituals, myths, and customs of the Egyptians that still persisted in their day.

# 2 THE FUNCTIONS OF EGYPTIAN MYTHOLOGY

When dealing with any ancient culture, it is impossible to know how much of its worship was sincere and how much was driven by custom and politics. It was to the benefit of the pharaohs, after all, to emphasize the power of the gods and link it to their own power. It was also to their benefit to have the rest of the population see them as infallible and divine. At the same time, the presence of shrines and smaller temples all over Egypt tell us of daily prayers and offerings to ward off sickness, bring blessings, and thank the gods for their gifts.

We have to use what knowledge we have of Egypt to make educated guesses about the roles its myths played in ceremony and daily life. We simply have to remember that even the best guesses may fall short of the mark or be

**This "reserve head" replaced the decayed head of a mummy in a tomb near Giza, Egypt.**

completely changed by the discovery of a previously unknown arti-
fact or record. When examining ancient cultures, we have to
respect their complexity and try to avoid making assumptions
based on the cultures with which we are more familiar.

# The Foundations of Egyptian Mythology

Egyptian mythology was ultimately centered around the pharaoh. It
was the pharaoh who was the embodiment of the great god Horus
and, to some extent, of the god Ra himself. After his death, the
pharaoh was also called Osiris, after the god of the underworld, who
had once been a human king and whom the pharaoh would repre-
sent in the afterlife. It was the pharaoh's job to oversee all of Egypt,
to ensure that the gods were given proper respect, that grain was
stored up for the lean years, that armies were raised when needed,
and that great temples and monuments were built.

Another underpinning of Egyptian mythology was the cycle of
the Nile. A life-giving oasis in the midst of a harsh desert, the Nile
made civilization in Egypt possible. And although there are many
myths about the deeds of the pharaohs, there is also the myth of
Khnemu, also spelled Khnum, of the Nile, which we will discuss in
chapter 5. Khnemu of the Nile was a god who had to be appeased in
order for the Nile to flourish. The pharaoh symbolized power, but
the Nile symbolized life itself.

Compared to many of the neighboring cultures, ancient Egypt
was remarkably stable and slow to change. The predictable bounty

This fresco in the tomb of Queen Nefertari shows the god Ra and other divinities. Frescos such as these, along with numerous other objects, are examples of artifacts that ancient Egyptians buried with their dead. Their belief in the afterlife was strong, so they supplied the dead with many earthly relics to help them along their way into the next world.

of the Nile and the surrounding desert that helped protect Egypt from invaders may explain why Egypt's pharaohs seemed to face little internal strife. Egypt did muster armies against invaders and occasionally seized land from its neighbors to enlarge its empire, but it never attempted conquest on the scale of the Greeks or Romans. Perhaps the hearts of its people were tied too closely to the Nile and its prosperity to be driven to seek out new and strange homes. So long as most Egyptians remained content with things as they were, there was no need to question the power of the pharaoh or the ways of their gods.

So it is in the fertility, isolation, and relative stability of Egyptian society that we can set the foundations of its mythology. Egyptian mythology was often concerned with family squabbles over power, the battles between men and women, and the importance of honoring the gods and behaving properly for one's social standing. Stories of great battles, like that of *The Iliad*, the Greek epic recounting the Trojan War, were rare compared to colorful tales about lost sailors or conniving women.

## Mythology and the Afterlife

There is one element of Egypt's mythology that dominates all the rest: its obsession with the afterlife. This fixation fueled Egypt's greatest architecture and absorbed enormous amounts of its wealth and energy. Some of the earliest Egyptian settlements show evidence of the burial of the dead with the necessities of life—clothes, jewelry, cosmetics, food, and water. This trend intensified as time passed. Tombs became more and more elaborate, filled with every possible tool and luxury that the deceased might need in the afterlife. The invention of the mummification process allowed the body itself to be somewhat preserved. Eventually, detailed copies of the Book of the Dead, which included instructions for how to successfully navigate the afterlife, were carefully entombed with the deceased.

In order for there to be an afterlife, there must be a part of the individual that survives death. The Egyptians believed that the Ba was everything, except the body, that made a person an individual and unique. The Ka was the "double" of a person, which journeyed to the underworld after death to be judged and

**People from all social classes in ancient Egypt believed in the afterlife. As a testament to this, they buried their dead with items from this world to help them on their way into the next. Shown on top is a wooden box with jewelry from the tomb of a girl. Below this is a game board from the tomb of King Tutankhamen.**

perhaps admitted into the presence of the gods. The Akh was the reunified Ka and Ba, which would also be part of the Akh-Akh, all the other Akhs of humanity and of animals, in the afterlife.

All mythologies and societies concern themselves with death to some degree. But only among Egypt's nobility were the living so focused on the afterlife that building a tomb and filling it with treasure took up so much of their resources.

Egypt had no great public buildings, aside from tombs and temples. Everything else, even the homes of the wealthy and government buildings, was made of mud brick, which quickly erodes. The pyramids, the most famous monuments of ancient Egypt, were dwellings for life in another world, not this one.

But while this preoccupation with the afterlife can make the Egyptians seem like a gloomy people, the texts and hieroglyphs they left

**Shown here are the great Pyramids of Giza. They are, from left to right, the pyramids of Mycerinus, Khafre, and Cheops. These pyramids date from the twenty-sixth century BC. The inset shows the tomb of Ramses VI and his sarcophagus (stone coffin), located in the Valley of the Kings.**

behind show a people with a great capacity for pleasure, which included hunting, dancing, and eating with abandon. Perhaps the Egyptians' focus on the next world was not out of a sense of doom but out of a desire to keep the pleasures of this world going on forever, without interruption.

# 3 THE WORLD OF THE EGYPTIAN GODS

The Egyptian gods were, like all gods, connected to the world of those who worshipped them. They symbolized both the natural world (the sun, the animals, the sky, the Nile) and more abstract ideas such as death, justice, and honor.

This stone carving of a baboon is from the main gate of a former temple of the moon god Thoth.

There are literally hundreds of gods and goddesses in the entire Egyptian pantheon. Many are local gods of the hearth and field, or different aspects of the same gods in different villages. The identities of the gods could blur as old gods fell out of favor and new ones arose to take their places and their attributes. While this posed no problem to ancient Egyptians, it can make things difficult for modern researchers attempting to categorize all the names, powers, and roles of each god and goddess, and to see Egyptian mythology as a single, coherent system.

# Gods and Goddesses

While a list of all the Egyptian gods would be too long for our purposes, we can touch here on the most important gods and goddesses and the roles they played in Egyptian society.

## Ra

Ra, also known as Re or Amun-Ra, was believed to be the primary creator god (although the followers of Khnemu and Ptah sometimes contested this, insisting their god was the primary one). In the simplest terms, Ra represented the sun. He sailed through the sky each day in his sky boat and then through the underworld in his night boat. He was born out of Nun, the great primeval ocean and created the rest of the early gods, the earth, and humankind.

Ra can be portrayed as a hawk or hawk-headed man, like Horus, or as the sun itself, among other manifestations. While the pharaoh did not embody Ra, he was considered to be like Ra in his absolute power. Egyptian nobility built many temples and shrines to this father of the gods.

## Osiris

Once a human pharaoh, Osiris was said to be the man, the first pharaoh, who taught humans agriculture, science, and the arts after gaining his knowledge from the great god Thoth. After his murder and

As in many depictions in which he is holding kingship staffs and is bearded, Osiris dominates this wall painting in the tomb of Sennutem in the Deir el-Medina cemetery. Osiris was one of the most important gods in Egyptian mythology and one of the most versatile in terms of his powers. He was both the god of fertility as well as the embodiment of the dead and the resurrected king.

Isis, shown at right, was the supreme goddess. In this wall painting from the tomb of Horemheb, the last king of the Eighteenth Dynasty, she is facing Horemheb himself. Isis's name is associated with the hieroglyph for throne.

resurrection, he did not fully return to the world of the living but instead became lord of the underworld, allowing his son Horus to rule on Earth.

Osiris's death and resurrection were associated with the rise and fall of the Nile, as well as with the daily travels of Ra through the sky and the underworld. His rivalry with his brother Seth, who became the god of storms and the desert, was a symbol of the struggle between the fertile land of the Nile and the surrounding harshness of the desert. Osiris is usually portrayed as a bearded, mummified man with green skin, holding the staffs associated with kingship.

## Isis

The greatest of the goddesses, Isis was the wife of Osiris. It was she who brought him back from the dead after his murder by his brother Seth. She also protected their son, Horus, until he could assume his father's place. In fact, it was through a clever trick by Isis that Horus was given his power and his place among the gods. As the mother of Horus, she was also considered the protector of the pharaoh, who embodied him. She is often depicted wearing a solar disk between a pair of horns, holding an infant Horus on her lap. The symbol for her name was also associated with the symbol for the throne of Egypt itself.

## Bes

A dwarf god who guarded against evil spirits and misfortune, Bes was the protector of the pharaohs and a god of children, pleasure, music, and dance. He protected homes through such tasks as killing snakes, fighting off evil spirits, watching after children, encouraging fertility, and aiding women in labor. His image was kept in many homes to ward off evil. It is thought that he may have been imported from Nubia during the period of the Middle Kingdom.

## Thoth

Thoth was the god of the moon (a title he shared with some other gods), wisdom, writing, magic,

**Bes, shown here in a stone carving at the Temple of Hathor in Dendera, Egypt, is represented, as usual, as a dwarf. He is often presented as a comical figure and was known to bring out joy and drive away sadness. He was often portrayed on mirrors, ointment vases, and other personal items.**

This painted stone relief (a kind of sculpture) is of the god Thoth with Seti I from the Nineteenth Dynasty. This wall painting is in the tomb of Seti I. Seti I, son of Ramses I, is believed by many scholars to have been the greatest king of the Nineteenth Dynasty. He greatly promoted the advancement of Egypt with the building of quarries, wells, and temples.

and the measurement of time, among other things. He was a son of either Ra or Seth, but he was also said to be the secretary and counselor of Ra. In the underworld, he helped Osiris judge the souls of the dead. He is usually depicted with the head of a baboon or that of an ibis (a bird whose beak is the shape of a crescent moon).

## Seth

Seth, sometimes spelled "Set," was the god of chaotic forces, which are represented by war, storms, foreign lands (and foreigners), and deserts. He protected desert caravans but also caused sandstorms. Seth protected Ra as Ra journeyed through the land of the dead every night. He also killed Apep, also known as Apophis, the evil serpent of darkness who attacked Ra each night. When Seth's brother, Osiris, became a more important god, Seth came to be seen as his opponent. Seth eventually killed Osiris in their struggle and spread the pieces of Osiris's body over Egypt, becoming a god of evil (and thieves). Seth is depicted with square ears, a forked tail, and

The god Seth is shown on the left of this limestone stela of Aapehty. Aapehty was the deputy of a gang of workers who fashioned the royal tombs. Seth is shown in his classic form with squared ears and curved snout. This composite of man and beast is what Egyptologists call the "Seth animal."

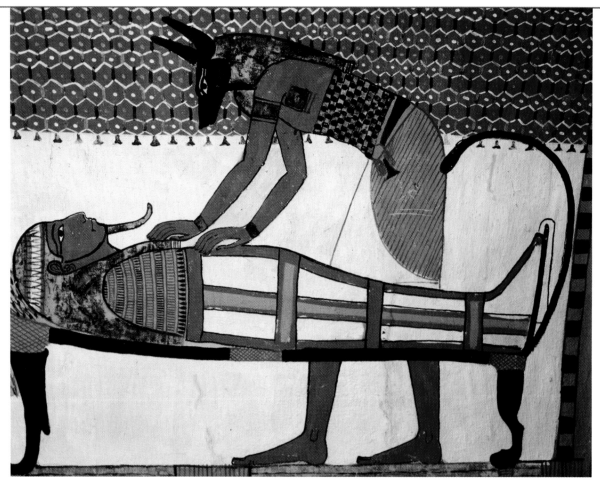

**Anubis and a mummy are represented on this mural from the Tomb of Sennedjem. As the god of death and dying, Anubis is shown preparing the mummy for its passage into the afterlife.**

a curved snout. Some people believe the animal represented was an aardvark or a type of pig. Seth was also associated with gazelles, donkeys, crocodiles, and hippopotamuses.

## Anubis

Anubis was the god of death and dying, and before Osiris's arrival, god of the underworld. He has the head of a jackal, since the jackal is a scavenger of the dead. He was also known as the Guardian of the Dead. His role was primarily that of either holding or watching the scales with which the hearts of the dead were weighed against the feather of Ma'at. The heart was believed to contain the intelligence and memory of the individual, and therefore bore the record of the person's life. If the heart was as light as the feather, Anubis led it to Osiris. Otherwise, it was fed to Ammit, the goddess of destruction, and the heart would be devoured and forbidden to continue its journey to Osiris. Anubis also guarded the physical remains of bodies and tombs, where his image is often found.

# 4 THE PEASANT WHO BECAME KING, THE PRINCESS OF BEKHTEN, AND THE GOLDEN LOTUS

The following myths are only a sample of Egypt's rich mythology illustrating some of the concerns the ancient Egyptians had about the roles of men and women, the proper places of kings and commoners, and the importance of honoring the wishes of the gods. At the same time, they are tales of adventure, romance, deceit, heroism, and wonder, which entertained listeners rich and poor.

## The Peasant Who Became King

*There were once two brothers, the older named Anpu, also known as Anubis, and the younger Bata. Bata lived*

Shown here is the Temple of Khonsu from the time of the New Kingdom in the Twentieth Dynasty.

with Anpu and Anpu's wife, and worked for them in the fields. Bata was a very virtuous man.

One day, Anpu's wife made romantic advances toward Bata, which he refused. She then told Anpu that Bata had attacked her, and Anpu pursued his brother. Bata told his side of the story and wounded himself to prove his sincerity to his brother.

Anpu believed his brother and was stricken with grief. Bata said, "My soul will leave my body and dwell in the highest blossom of the acacia tree. When the tree is cut down, my soul will fall upon the ground. There you may find it and must place it in a vessel of water and I shall come to life again. When the hour comes, your beer will bubble and your wine will have a foul smell. I am going to live in the valley of the flowering acacia."

Then Anpu returned home, killed his wife, and went into mourning. Bata traveled to the valley of the acacia. He met nine gods, who took pity on him and decided to make him a bride of his own, more beautiful than any other woman, and Bata loved her dearly. He told her where his soul was kept and all his secrets.

One day, Bata's wife went out to walk below the acacia. The sea spirit saw her and pursued her, and she ran back home. The spirit complained of his love for her, and the acacia tree gave him a lock of her hair, which he took and let float away to the land of Egypt. It floated into the place where the king's washers washed their master's garments and perfumed them. The washers did not understand how the clothes had

This limestone wall painting from the tomb of Khnumhotep III is from the Twelfth Dynasty. It shows acacia trees, prominent in Egyptian mythology, as symbols of birth. The Egyptian gods are said to have been born under the goddess Saosis's acacia tree. In later legends, the acacia tree is also a symbol of death and the afterlife.

become perfumed. Finally, the chief washer discovered the lock of hair and took it to the king. The king summoned his scribes, who declared that the lock must be from a divine daughter of Ra in the land of the flowering acacia and that he should send his men to search for her.

But Bata slew all the king's men when they came to his valley. Then the king sent forth more messengers and soldiers, and also a woman laden with jewelry. The wife of Bata decided to go with the king's men. She then told the king the secret of Bata's soul's hiding place. The king decreed, "Let the acacia be cut down and splintered in pieces." The task was carried out because the king didn't want any competition over her, and Bata dropped dead.

Meanwhile Anpu's beer bubbled, and his wine had a foul smell. He hastened to the house of Bata and found him lying dead. After a long search for Bata's soul, he found an acacia seed and dropped it in a pitcher of water and poured it in Bata's mouth. Bata then came back to life.

Bata said, "Now I will become a sacred bull. Lead me before the king." Anpu delivered the bull to the king and returned home. When Bata's former wife walked by, the bull said to her, "I am still alive." "Who are you?" she asked. "I am Bata. It was you who tried to kill me. But I live on." Bata's former wife trembled and ran away.

That night she told the king, "I want to eat the liver of the sacred bull." The king ordered that the bull be sacrificed. It was, and two great trees grew where the bull's blood fell. One

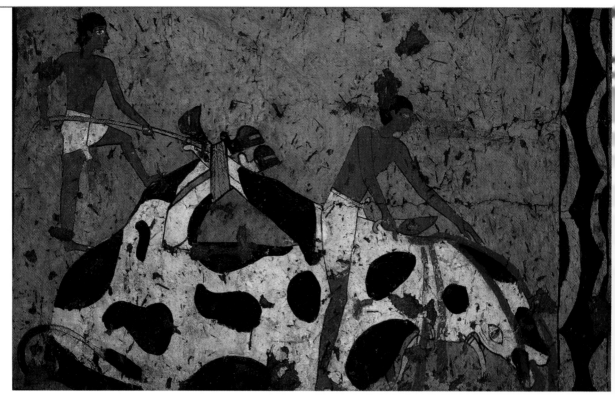

This fresco is from the tomb of Iti from the Middle Kingdom of around 2000 BC. It shows the slaughtering of a captured bull. In "The Peasant Who Became King," Bata became a sacred bull that was eventually slaughtered and whose blood turned into the acacia trees.

*day, Bata's former wife walked beneath the trees and heard them whisper, "It is me, Bata. False woman, I am still alive!"*

*She went to the king and asked him to have the trees cut down. He agreed, and she went to watch the woodsmen fell them. As she stood there, a small chip of wood entered her mouth, and she swallowed it. Soon after, she gave birth to a son, whom the king named his heir, assuming the child was his. But the child was actually Bata reborn.*

*The old king died, and the child grew into a man and became the king. One day, he said, "Summon before me the great men of my court, so that I may now reveal the truth concerning the queen."*

*His unfaithful wife was brought before him and judged. Then Anpu was summoned and chosen to be the royal heir. When Bata died after reigning for thirty years, his brother was made the new king.*

# The Princess of Bekhten

*Ramses II was in the country of Nehern, collecting tribute in the form of gifts according to an annual custom, when the prince of Bekhten came with the other chiefs to salute Ramses and offer him gold, lapis lazuli, turquoise, and precious woods. The prince also brought with his offerings his eldest daughter, who was exceedingly beautiful. Ramses accepted the maiden and took her to Egypt, where he made her the chief royal wife and gave her the name of Ra-neferu, or "the beauties of Ra."*

*Some time after, the prince of Bekhten appeared in Thebes and paid homage to the king. He then explained that he had come on behalf of the young sister of Ra-neferu, who was very ill, and begged the king to send a physician to see her. The king summoned all the learned men of his court, and the royal scribe Tehuti-em-beb was selected to go. When Tehuti-em-beb arrived in Bekhten, he found the princess was under the influence of an evil spirit, which he could not defeat. The king of Bekhten sent another envoy to Ramses, asking him to send a god to heal his daughter, and the envoy arrived in Thebes at the time when the*

Ramses II, who is characterized in "The Princess of Bekhten," is depicted here in this black granite statue. He was the third king of the Nineteenth Dynasty, ruling from 1279 to 1213 BC. His was the second-longest reign in Egyptian history, during which he initiated many building programs, including statues of himself all over Egypt.

*king was celebrating the festival of Amon, the god of Thebes.*

*As soon as the king had heard what was wanted, he went into the temple of Khonsu Nefer-hetep (one of the gods of the moon) and said, "Oh, my fair lord, I have come once again into thy presence to ask your help for the daughter of the prince of Bekhten." The god answered his prayer and agreed to go to Bekhten with the envoy.*

*As soon as he had been welcomed to the country by the prince of Bekhten and his generals and nobles, the god went to the princess and healed her of the demon. The demon spoke to Khonsu, acknowledged his power, and promised to*

Shown here is a contemporary photo of the Temple of Khonsu. The temple was constructed during the ruling periods of both Ramses III and Ramses IV. It is located in the religious center of Karnak, which is in the northern part of the ancient Egyptian capital of Thebes.

*depart, but he begged Khonsu to ask the prince of Bekhten to make a feast at which they both might be present. He did so, and the god, the demon, and the prince spent a very happy day together. When the feast concluded, the demon returned to his own land according to his promise.*

*The prince wished to keep Khonsu in Bekhten and persuaded him to stay for three years, four months, and five days, but eventually Khonsu returned to Egypt in the form of a hawk of gold. In thanks for all he had done, the king of Bekhten sent a chariot back to Egypt loaded with gifts and offerings of every kind. On his return, Khonsu took all the gifts that had been given to him and carried them to his temple. Ever after, the priests of Khonsu spoke of their god "who could perform mighty deeds and miracles, and vanquish the demons of darkness."*

# The Golden Lotus

*One day, Pharaoh Snefru wandered wearily through his palace, bored. He called his chief magician, Zazamankh, and said, "Devise something that will fill my heart with pleasure." Zazamankh replied, "Oh, Pharaoh, life, health, strength be to you! My counsel is that you go sailing upon the Nile, and upon the lake below Memphis. This will be no common voyage, if you will follow my advice."*

*"Believing that you will show me marvels, I will order out the Royal Boat," said Snefru. "Yet I am weary of sailing upon the Nile and upon the lake."*

*"This will be no common voyage," Zazamankh assured him. "For your rowers will be fair maidens from the Royal House of the King's Women, and as you watch them rowing and see the birds upon the lake, and the sweet fields and the green grass upon the banks, your heart will grow glad."*

*At this, the pharaoh became interested, and he gave his magician permission to order everything he needed. Then Zazamankh ordered twenty oars of ebony inlaid with gold,*

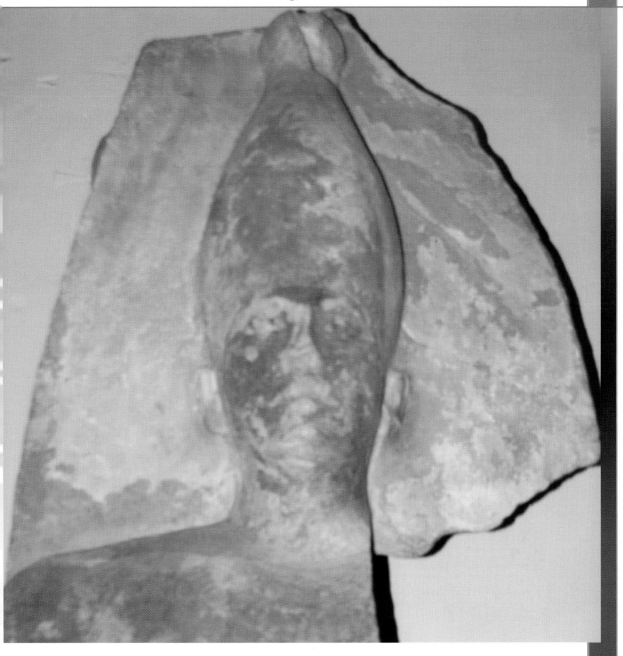

This is a stone carving of the pharaoh Snefru, from "The Golden Lotus." Snefru came to power in the twenty-fifth century BC. He was responsible for initiating commerce across the sea with Phoenicia. He also traded cedar with Lebanon and used the wood to build ships nearly 170 feet (50 meters) long, which sailed on the Nile. He established Egypt's power in the Sinai Peninsula, a major center of copper production.

with blades of wood inlaid with electrum, and the twenty fairest maidens in the pharaoh's household as rowers. He also ordered twenty nets of golden thread to be the maiden's garments and ornaments of gold, electrum, and malachite for them.

All was done according to the words of Zazamankh, and presently the pharaoh was seated in the Royal Boat while the maidens rowed him up and down the stream. Snefru's heart was glad at the sight.

But presently, one of the maidens steering the boat lost the golden lotus she wore in her hair when it fell into the water. She cried out and stopped singing, which caused the maidens to stop rowing. "Why have you ceased to steer and lead the rowers with your song?" asked Snefru.

"Forgive me, Pharaoh—life, health, strength be to you!" she sobbed. "But I have lost the beautiful golden lotus that your majesty gave to me, and it has fallen into the river."

Then the pharaoh said, "There is only one who can find a golden lotus that has sunk to the bottom of the lake. Bring Zazamankh to me." So Zazamankh came, and the pharaoh told him what he wished to be done. "Pharaoh, my lord," answered Zazamankh, "I will do what you ask, and it will be an enchantment you have never seen, and it will fill you with wonder, even as I promised."

Zazamankh stood at the stern of the Royal Boat and began to chant great words of power. And as he did this, the lake parted as if a piece had been cut out of it with a great sword. The lake here was 20 feet (6.1 m) deep, and the water *that the magician moved rose up and set itself upon the surface of the lake so that there was a cliff of water on that side 40 feet (12.2 m) high.*

*Now the Royal Boat slid gently down into the great cleft in the lake until it rested on the bottom. On the side toward the 40-foot (12.2 m) cliff of water, there was a great open space where the bottom of the lake lay uncovered, as firm and dry as the land itself. And there, just below the stern of the Royal Boat, lay the golden lotus.*

*With a cry of joy, the maiden who had lost it sprang over the side onto the firm ground, picked it up, and set it once more in her hair. Then she climbed swiftly back into the Royal Boat and took the steering oar into her hands once more. The Royal Boat slid up the side of the water until it was level with the surface once more. Then, at another word of power, the great piece of water slid back into place, and the evening breeze rippled the still surface of the lake as if nothing out of the ordinary had happened.*

*But the heart of Snefru rejoiced and was filled with wonder, and he cried, "Zazamankh, my brother, you are the greatest and wisest of magicians! You have shown me wonders and delights this day, and your reward shall be all that you desire and a place next to my own in Egypt." Then the Royal Boat sailed gently on over the lake in the glow of the evening, while the twenty lovely maidens dipped their ebony and silver oars in the shimmering waters and sang sweetly a love song of old Egypt.*

# 5 THE MYTH OF RA AND ISIS, THE BOOK OF THOTH, AND THE SEVEN YEARS' FAMINE

This second set of myths addresses the ancient themes of power, including that of the gods that existed in daily Egyptian life and that of knowledge. The strength of these myths is evidenced in their longevity. Not only were they central to ancient Egyptians, their lessons are as powerful today as they were thousands of years ago.

## The Myth of Ra and Isis

*The goddess Isis was powerful, but one day she began to wonder, "Why can't I be as powerful as Ra?" Now Ra had grown*

Shown here is a statue of Ptah holding a scepter. On the scepter is an ankh, a loop symbolizing life, and four horizontal *djed* pillars, which symbolize stability.

The goddess Isis is shown here carved in basalt stone from the tomb of
Ramses III. Known for her power, wisdom, and magical abilities, Isis was
believed to be the personification of the throne.

*old, and as he walked, he drooled on the earth. Isis kneaded the wet earth, formed a cobra from it, and let it lie in the path that Ra would take each day.*

*The next day, Ra was bitten by the cobra, and he was poisoned. He cried out and fell down, but none of the other gods was able to help him. Then Isis came and offered to use her words of power to heal him. "But you must tell me your true name. For he shall live whose name shall be revealed."*

*At first Ra would not say his name, but the poison kept spreading deeper and deeper, and he could not fight it. Finally, he consented to let Isis search through his body for his secret name, and she healed him of the poison. Ever after, she was the most powerful of the goddesses and became widely known for her wisdom and magic.*

## The Book of Thoth

*Once there was a prince of Egypt called Setna who was a great magician. While the other princes spent their days hunting or leading their fathers' armies, Setna was never so happy as when left alone to study.*

*He was a magician whom none could surpass, for he had learned his art from the most secret of the ancient writings, which even the priests of Amen-Re, Ptah, and Thoth could not read.*

*One day, he came upon the story of another pharaoh's son, who was as great a scribe and as wise a magician as he. He was greater and wiser, indeed, for Nefrekeptah had read The Book of*

This Second-Dynasty tomb painting depicts the recently deceased standing before Osiris, Isis, and Thoth. Thoth is the figure with the crescent-shaped beak. Behind Thoth is Isis, and in the back is Osiris.

*Thoth, which taught a man how to enchant both heaven and earth, as well as the language of the birds and beasts.*

*When Setna read that The Book of Thoth had been buried with Nefrekeptah in his royal tomb at Memphis, he was determined to find and read it. He asked his brother, Anherru, to go with him. The two brothers set out for Memphis, and it was not hard for them to find the tomb of Nefrekeptah.*

*At the tomb, Setna found the body of the prince lying wrapped in linen bands. Beside the body, on the stone sarcophagus, sat two ghostly figures, the Kas of a beautiful young woman and a boy. And between them, on the dead breast of Nefrekeptah, lay The Book of Thoth.*

*Setna bowed to the two Kas and said, "May Osiris have you in his keeping. Know that I am Setna, the priest of Ptah, son of Ramses I, the greatest pharaoh of all—and I come for The Book of Thoth. I beg you to let me take it in peace, for if not I have the power to take it by force or magic."*

*Then the woman Ka told him that she and the other spirit were Ahura and Merab, the wife and son of Nefrekeptah, whose bodies were buried elsewhere. She told him a terrible tale, how she and her family were happy until the day her husband heard a priest mention The Book of Thoth, with all its power over heaven and earth. Nefrekeptah paid the priest a great deal of silver to learn the hiding place of the book. It was hidden in the middle of the Nile, inside three boxes, guarded by snakes, scorpions, and a great immortal serpent.*

*With his great knowledge of magic, Nefrekeptah was able to defeat the serpent and take the book. But as he and his family set sail for home, his son was seized by an enchantment by the god Thoth and fell into the river and drowned. Later, his wife died in the same way, and both were buried in Koptos.*

When Nefrekeptah himself arrived in Memphis, he was found dead with The Book of Thoth bound to his chest, and he was buried with it. Then the Kas of his son and wife came to watch over him, where Setna saw them now.

"And now I have told you all the woe that has befallen us because my husband took and read The Book of Thoth—the book which you ask him to give up. It is not yours, you have no claim to it. Indeed, for the sake of it, we gave up our lives on earth," said Ahura.

But Setna was still determined to have the book. As he went to seize it, the Ka of Nefrekeptah arose and said, "Setna, if after hearing my tale, yet you will take no warning, then The Book of Thoth must be yours. But first you must win it from me by playing a game of dice. Do you accept?" Setna agreed, and the game began. Nefrekeptah won the first game from Setna,

Ptah, shown here, is holding a scepter carved with the symbols of life *(ankh)*, power *(was)*, and stability *(djed)*. Ptah divided his labor with the funerary god Sokar. Ptah was associated with stonework. Sokar was associated with metalwork.

who promptly sank into the ground above the ankles. Setna lost the second game and sank to his waist in the ground. When Setna lost a third time, he sank up to his neck. But he cried out to his brother, Anherru, who stood outside the tomb, "Run to the pharaoh and get the amulet of Ptah, to save me!"

Anherru did so, and when he returned, he used the amulet's power to free Setna from Nefrekeptah's spells. Setna sprang out of the ground, snatched The Book of Thoth from Nefrekeptah's body, and fled with Anherru from the tomb.

As they went, they heard the Ka of Nefrekeptah say, "I will make Setna bring back The Book of Thoth and come as a suppliant to my tomb with a forked stick in his hand and a fire-pan on his head." Once Setna and Anherru were outside, the tomb closed behind them and seemed as if it had never been opened.

When Setna stood before his father the great pharaoh and told him all that had happened and returned the amulet of Ptah, his father counseled him to take the book back, but Setna refused. Instead, he spent all his time reading The Book of Thoth and studying all the spells contained in it. And often he would carry it into the Temple of Ptah and read from it to those who sought his wisdom.

One day, he saw a beautiful maiden who knelt to make her offerings before the statue of Ptah. Soon he learned that she was called Tabubua, and she was the daughter of the high priest of the cat goddess Bastet. He fell in love and forgot all else, even The Book of Thoth. He sent a message to her, and they arranged to meet secretly at her palace in the desert.

*There Tabubua welcomed him, led him to her chamber, and served him wine in a golden cup.*

*He professed his love, and she replied that she would return it if he would divorce his wife and leave his own children in poverty. He agreed, but when he went to embrace her, he found that she had transformed into a hideous withered corpse.*

*Setna cried out in terror and fainted. He awoke lying naked in the desert beside the road to Memphis. The passersby on the road mocked Setna. But one kinder than the rest threw him an old cloak, and with this about him, he came back to Memphis like a beggar.*

*When he reached his home and found his wife and children there alive and well, he decided to return The Book of Thoth to Nefrekeptah. "If Tabubua was but a dream," he exclaimed, "they show me in what terrible danger I stand. For if another spell is cast upon me, next time it will prove to be no dream."*

*So Setna took the book back to the Nefrekeptah, carrying a forked stick and a fire-pan on his head as a suppliant. Nefrekeptah's Ka laughed, saying, "I told you that you would return. Place it upon my body where it lay these many years. But do not think that you are yet free of my vengeance. Unless you do as I say, the dream of Tabubua will be turned into reality."*

*Setna, terrified, agreed. As Nefrekeptah asked, Setna searched for and found the bodies of Ahura and Merab, and had them transferred to Nefrekeptah's tomb. After the ceremonies, Setna spoke a charm, and the wall of the tomb closed behind him, leaving no trace of a door. Then, at the pharaoh's command,*

The Island of Elephantine, or Elephantine Island, is referenced in "The Seven Years' Famine." Shown in this modern photograph, Elephantine Island is the oldest prehistoric Egyptian community. In the late 1960s, the island was chosen as a site for archaeological excavations to discover the lifestyle in ancient Egyptian cities. It was chosen because civilization on the island dates back to the late prehistoric period.

*they heaped sand over the low stone shrine where the entrance to the tomb was hidden. Before long, a sandstorm hid the tomb so that never again could anyone find The Book of Thoth.*

# The Seven Years' Famine

*In the eighteenth year of the king Tcheser, also known as Djoser (the third king of the Third Dynasty), the whole region*

*of the south, the Island of Elephantine, and the district of Nubia were ruled by a high official named Mater. The king sent Mater a dispatch asking for his help because for seven years there had not been enough flooding to produce good crops. Grain of every kind was very scarce, and the people had*

**One of the goddesses in "The Seven Years' Famine" was Nut, shown here. In this detail of Nut on a painted Egyptian coffin, she is shown spreading her wings in protection over the deceased.**

*very little food to eat and were in such need that men were robbing their neighbors. Men wished to walk but could not do so for want of strength. Children were crying for food, and the aged lay themselves down on the ground to die.*

*In this terrible trouble, King Tcheser asked his governor Mater to tell him where the Nile rose and who the tutelary god or goddess of it was. Mater made his way immediately to the king with an answer. He told the king that the Nile flood came forth from the Island of Elephantine, on which the first city that ever existed stood. The spot on the island out of which the river rose was the double cavern Qerti. This double cavern was, in fact, the "couch of the Nile," and from it the*

Khnemu, also known as Khnum, appears in this carving from the wall of the Temple of Khnum. Khnemu was a creator god. Using his potter's wheel, he made the bodies of both gods and humans. Shown here as he is often depicted, Khnemu bears the head of a ram.

*Nile god watched until the season of inundation drew near, and then he rushed forth like a vigorous young man and filled the whole country. The guardian of this flood was Khnemu, and it was he who kept the doors that held it in and who drew back the bolts at the proper time.*

*Mater next went on to describe the temple of Khnemu at Elephantine and told his royal master that the other gods were Sept (Sothis or Satis), Anqet (Anukis), Hapi, Shu, Geb, Nut, Osiris, Horus, Isis, and Nephthys. After this, he enumerated the various products that were found in the neighborhood and which offerings ought to be made for Khnemu. When the king heard these words, he offered sacrifices to the god and, in due course, went into his temple to make supplication before him.*

*Finally, Khnemu appeared before him and promised that the Nile should rise every year, as in olden times, and described the good which should come upon the land when he had made an end of the famine. When Khnemu ceased to speak, King Tcheser remembered that the god had complained that no one took the trouble to repair his shrine, even though stone lay near in abundance. He immediately issued a decree in which he ordered that certain lands on each side of the Nile near Elephantine to be set apart for the endowment of the temple of Khnemu and that a certain tax should be levied upon every product of the neighborhood and be devoted to the maintenance of the priesthood of the god. The original text of the decree was written upon wood, and as this was not lasting, the king ordered that a copy of it should be cut upon a stone stela, which should be set in a prominent place.*

# Ancient Myths in a Modern World

Ancient Egyptian mythologies teach us that the struggles we face—deciding who rules, maintaining order, describing and understanding the world around us and our fellow human beings, dealing with the mystery and inevitability of death—are very old struggles. All human societies have wrestled with these issues in their own ways. And while Egypt's mythology died out after the Egyptian Empire declined, the myths and artifacts the people left behind tell us of a strong, vibrant culture that still has lessons to teach us.

Modern Egypt is a very different place. After the great pharaonic dynasties died out in about 1075 BC, the region became a colony of the Nubians, then the Greeks, then the Roman Empire. During this period of chaos and upheaval, innumerable ties to the language and literature of ancient Egypt were lost or destroyed. Before the science of archaeology existed, generations of neglect and theft destroyed many precious records and artifacts. But since the nineteenth century, more and better ways of preserving the past continue to be discovered. Modern Egyptians now take a proud view of their heritage and have passed many laws regulating how excavations are performed and protecting their rights to their own history.

Ancient Egyptians struggled, created, lived, loved, and died much as we do. The myths and gods of the Egyptians helped them understand the unknown but also the everyday, the mysteries of birth and death but also the sunrise, the growing crops, and the hawks circling in the sky above. While we can't make too many assumptions about what this ancient people actually thought and believed, we know that they were people like us, trying to make sense of their world, as all people have and as we still do.

# GLOSSARY

**acacia**  A small tree or shrub native to Egypt with white or yellow flowers, associated with the gods, birth, and death.

**archaeologist**  One who studies the artifacts left behind by human civilizations.

**dynasty**  A powerful group or family that maintains its power for a long period of time.

**electrum**  A pale metal made of gold and silver.

**hieroglyphs**  Writing done in a style that uses pictures instead of letters or words, especially the ancient Egyptian system of writing.

**lapis lazuli**  A semiprecious stone that is a rich blue color, heavily worn by ancient Egyptian nobility.

**lotus**  A water lily native to Egypt; considered a symbol of the afterlife by the ancient Egyptians.

**malachite**  A green mineral used mainly for ornamental objects.

**oasis**  A fertile or green area in the midst of a dry or desert area.

**pantheon**  The gods of a people, especially the officially recognized gods.

**papyrus**  An early form of paper made from the papyrus reed, which was native to the Nile River valley.

**quarrying**  Digging or taking stone from an open excavation.

**stela**  A carved or inscribed stone or pillar used for ceremonial purposes.

**subsumed**  Placed within or included within something larger.

**suppliant**  A person who humbly asks for something.

# FOR MORE INFORMATION

Ancient Egypt Studies Association
P.O. Box 9805
Seattle, WA 98109
Web site: http://www.aesa-nw.org/index.html

Institute of Egyptian Art and Archaeology
University of Memphis
Jones Hall, Room 201
Memphis, TN 38152
(901) 678-2555
Web site: http://www.memphis.edu/egypt/main.html

## Web Sites

Due to the changing nature of Internet links, the Rosen Publishing Group, Inc., has developed an online list of Web sites related to the subject of this book. This site is updated regularly. Please use this link to access the list:

http://www.rosenlinks.com/maw/egyp

# FOR FURTHER READING

Harris, Geraldine. *Gods and Pharaohs from Egyptian Mythology* (The World Mythology Series). New York, NY: Peter Bedrick, 1993.

Morely, Jacqueline. *Egyptian Myths*. New York, NY: Peter Bedrick, 1999.

Nardo, Don, and William Sauts Bock. *Egyptian Mythology* (Mythology). Berkeley Heights, NJ: Enslow Publishers, 2001.

Sharukh, Husain. *Egypt* (Stories from Ancient Civilizations). Mankato, MN: Smart Apple Media, 2004.

Wilkinson, Richard H. *The Complete Gods and Goddesses of Ancient Egypt*. New York, NY: Thames & Hudson, 2003.

# BIBLIOGRAPHY

"Book of the Dead." Wikipedia.org. Retrieved April 2, 2005 (http://en.wikipedia.org/wiki/Book_of_the_Dead).

Carter, Howard, and A. C. Mace. *The Discovery of the Tomb of Tutankhamen*. New York, NY: Dover Publications, 1977.

Casson, Lionel. *Everyday Life in Ancient Egypt*. Baltimore, MD: The Johns Hopkins University Press, 2001.

David, Rosalie. *The Ancient Egyptians: Beliefs and Practices*. Portland, OR: Sussex Academic Press, 1998.

"Egyptian Book of Death." Aldokkan.com. Retrieved April 2, 2005 (http://www.aldokkan.com/religion/dead.htm).

"Egyptian Language." Answers.com. Retrieved April 2, 2005 (http://www.answers.com/topic/egyptian-language).

"Egyptian Mythology." Wikipedia.org. Retrieved April 2, 2005 (http://en.wikipedia.org/?title=Egyptian_mythology).

Green, Roger Lancelyn. *Tales of Ancient Egypt*. New York, NY: The Penguin Group, 2004.

Knight, Shawn C. "Introduction to Egyptology: Brief Biographies of Egyptian Gods." Sk4p.net. Retrieved April 2, 2005 (http://www.sk4p.net/egypt/gods.shtml).

"The Legend of Ra and Isis." Touregypt.net. Retrieved April 2, 2005 (http://www.touregypt.net/legendofraandisis.htm).

McDevitt, April. "The Book of Thoth." Ancient Egypt: The Mythology. Retrieved April 2, 2005 (http://www.egyptianmyths.net/mythbookthoth.htm).

McDevitt, April. "The Golden Lotus." Ancient Egypt: The Mythology. Retrieved April 2, 2005 (http://www.egyptianmyths.net/mythglotus.htm).

McDevitt, April. "The Myth of Bekhten." Ancient Egypt: The Mythology. Retrieved April 2, 2005 (http://www.egyptianmyths.net/mythbekhten.htm).

Shaw, Ian. *The Oxford History of Ancient Egypt*. New York, NY: Oxford University Press, 2000.

# ◼ INDEX

## About the Author

Janell Broyles is an editor and writer living in Brooklyn, New York. She had her first exposure to Middle Eastern culture and history while living in Saudi Arabia as a child. She focused much of her studies in college on ancient literatures and mythologies. This is her fourth book for the Rosen Publishing Group.

## Photo Credits

Designer: Thomas Forget
Editor: Nicholas Croce
Photo Researcher: Hillary Arnold